The Boxcar Children Mysteries

The Boxcar Children
Surprise Island
The Yellow House Mystery
Mystery Ranch
Mike's Mystery
Blue Bay Mystery
The Woodshed Mystery
The Lighthouse Mystery
Mountain Top Mystery
Schoolhouse Mystery
Caboose Mystery
Houseboat Mystery
Snowbound Mystery
Tree House Mystery
Bicycle Mystery
Mystery in the Sand
Mystery Behind the Wall
Bus Station Mystery
Benny Uncovers a Mystery
The Haunted Cabin Mystery
The Deserted Library Mystery
The Animal Shelter Mystery
The Old Motel Mystery
The Mystery of the Hidden Painting
The Amusement Park Mystery
The Mystery of the Mixed-Up Zoo
The Camp-Out Mystery
The Mystery Girl
The Mystery Cruise
The Disappearing Friend Mystery
The Mystery of the Singing Ghost
Mystery in the Snow
The Pizza Mystery
The Mystery Horse
The Mystery at the Dog Show
The Castle Mystery
The Mystery of the Lost Village
The Mystery on the Ice
The Mystery of the Purple Pool
The Ghost Ship Mystery
The Mystery in Washington, DC
The Canoe Trip Mystery
The Mystery of the Hidden Beach
The Mystery of the Missing Cat
The Mystery at Snowflake Inn
The Mystery on Stage
The Dinosaur Mystery
The Mystery of the Stolen Music
The Mystery at the Ball Park
The Chocolate Sundae Mystery
The Mystery of the Hot Air Balloon
The Mystery Bookstore
The Pilgrim Village Mystery
The Mystery of the Stolen Boxcar
The Mystery in the Cave
The Mystery on the Train
The Mystery at the Fair
The Mystery of the Lost Mine
The Guide Dog Mystery
The Hurricane Mystery
The Pet Shop Mystery
The Mystery of the Secret Message
The Firehouse Mystery
The Mystery in San Francisco
The Niagara Falls Mystery
The Mystery at the Alamo
The Outer Space Mystery
The Soccer Mystery
The Mystery in the Old Attic
The Growling Bear Mystery
The Mystery of the Lake Monster

THE MYSTERY AT PEACOCK HALL

THE WINDY CITY MYSTERY

THE BLACK PEARL MYSTERY

THE CEREAL BOX MYSTERY

THE PANTHER MYSTERY

THE MYSTERY OF THE QUEEN'S JEWELS

THE STOLEN SWORD MYSTERY

THE BASKETBALL MYSTERY

THE MOVIE STAR MYSTERY

THE MYSTERY OF THE PIRATE'S MAP

THE GHOST TOWN MYSTERY

THE MYSTERY OF THE BLACK RAVEN

THE MYSTERY IN THE MALL

THE MYSTERY IN NEW YORK

THE GYMNASTICS MYSTERY

THE POISON FROG MYSTERY

THE MYSTERY OF THE EMPTY SAFE

THE HOME RUN MYSTERY

THE GREAT BICYCLE RACE MYSTERY

THE MYSTERY OF THE WILD PONIES

THE MYSTERY IN THE COMPUTER GAME

THE MYSTERY AT THE CROOKED HOUSE

THE HOCKEY MYSTERY

THE MYSTERY OF THE MIDNIGHT DOG

THE MYSTERY OF THE SCREECH OWL

THE SUMMER CAMP MYSTERY

THE COPYCAT MYSTERY

THE HAUNTED CLOCK TOWER MYSTERY

THE MYSTERY OF THE TIGER'S EYE

THE DISAPPEARING STAIRCASE MYSTERY

THE MYSTERY ON BLIZZARD MOUNTAIN

THE MYSTERY OF THE SPIDER'S CLUE

THE CANDY FACTORY MYSTERY

THE MYSTERY OF THE MUMMY'S CURSE

THE MYSTERY OF THE STAR RUBY

THE STUFFED BEAR MYSTERY

THE MYSTERY OF ALLIGATOR SWAMP

THE MYSTERY AT SKELETON POINT

THE TATTLETALE MYSTERY

THE COMIC BOOK MYSTERY

THE GREAT SHARK MYSTERY

THE ICE CREAM MYSTERY

THE MIDNIGHT MYSTERY

THE MYSTERY IN THE FORTUNE COOKIE

THE BLACK WIDOW SPIDER MYSTERY

THE RADIO MYSTERY

THE MYSTERY OF THE RUNAWAY GHOST

THE FINDERS KEEPERS MYSTERY

THE MYSTERY OF THE HAUNTED BOXCAR

THE CLUE IN THE CORN MAZE

THE GHOST OF THE CHATTERING BONES

THE SWORD OF THE SILVER KNIGHT

THE GAME STORE MYSTERY

THE MYSTERY OF THE ORPHAN TRAIN

THE VANISHING PASSENGER

THE GIANT YO-YO MYSTERY

THE CREATURE IN OGOPOGO LAKE

THE ROCK 'N' ROLL MYSTERY

THE SECRET OF THE MASK

THE SECRET OF THE MASK

created by

GERTRUDE CHANDLER WARNER

DATE DUE *Series*

ALBERT WHITMAN & Company
Morton Grove, Illinois

The Secret of the Mask
created by Gertrude Chandler Warner;
illustrated by Robert Papp.

978-0-8075-5564-4 (hardcover)
978-0-8075-5565-1(paperback)

Cover art by Robert Papp.

For more information about Albert Whitman & Company,
visit our web site at www.albertwhitman.com.

Contents

Contents

THE SECRET OF THE MASK

CHAPTER 1

Rain, Rain, Go Away

A bolt of lightning ripped across the night sky.

"One, one-thousand," whispered a frightened voice.

"Two, one-thousand," whispered another.

"Three, one-thousand, four, one-thousand," counted four soft voices together.

"Five, one—"

Thunder shook the house.

The four Alden children huddled on Henry's bed, staring out the window. The storm

1

Irvin L. Young Memorial Library
Whitewater, Wisconsin

had awakened them in the middle of the night. Six-year-old Benny was the first to tip-toe to his big brother's room. Violet and Jessie soon followed, with Watch scampering close behind.

"Will this storm ruin everything?" asked Violet.

"We'll have to wait and see," Henry said.

"It can't rain tomorrow," said Benny. "It just *can't.*"

Watch whimpered. Benny patted the dog and hugged him tight.

Downstairs in the kitchen, boxes and baskets and buckets of old things stood near the back door. On top of them lay bright green and pink posters the children had made:

Boxcar Backyard Sale
Saturday and Sunday 10-4:00.
Toys, books, clothes,
and much, MUCH more!

For one whole week, the children had cleaned out their closets, drawers, and shelves. Into boxes went clothes that didn't fit. Into baskets went toys no longer used.

Into buckets went books no longer read. But there could be no yard sale if it was storming outside.

Another bolt of lightning turned the black sky bright. "One, one-thousand, two, one-thousand, three, one-thousand." They counted until the thunder boomed.

"The storm is coming closer," said Henry. "When it's right over our house, the lightning and thunder will come at the same time."

The children's hearts pounded as they watched and waited. Once, they had no home to protect them from storms. After their parents died, the children were supposed to live with their grandfather. But when they heard he was mean, they ran away.

It was during a storm like this that they found shelter in an old railroad car. The boxcar quickly became their home, and they lived in it until Grandfather found them. When they saw how nice he was, they came to live with him. Later, he surprised them by bringing the boxcar to the backyard so they could play in it whenever they liked.

Suddenly, a burst of lightning and clash of thunder came all at once. "Oh, no!" cried Benny, jumping under the covers with Watch. They made such a funny lump in the bed that everyone laughed.

After a while, the storm drifted so far away they could hardly hear it. Then, four tired children and one sleepy dog curled up on Henry's bed and fell fast asleep.

*****

The next morning, the yard sparkled with sunshine. The children ate a quick breakfast of cereal with milk and bananas, then washed their dishes and went to work.

Twelve-year-old Jessie piled their yard-sale signs onto a red wagon and tossed in a ball of string and a pair of scissors. "See you later," she said, hurrying off to hang the signs around the neighborhood.

Violet set up a table with a sign that read, "Violet's Tasty Treat Table" in the shade of the large oak tree. The ten-year-old spread out a red-and-white tablecloth. On this she

put a tall pitcher of lemonade, plastic cups, napkins, and two plates of fresh-baked cookies.

Henry began making a cashier's table out of a board he'd found in the alley. The fourteen-year-old slipped the claw end of his hammer under a few old nails and pulled them out. Then he rubbed sandpaper over the board, making it smooth so no one would get a splinter.

As Benny emptied the boxes, baskets, and buckets of their old things onto tables, a familiar black truck rattled down the alley. Sticking up in the back were a three-legged chair, a kitchen sink, one snow ski, and a lamp with a torn shade.

Everyone in Greenfield knew Mr. Robbins's truck. Every morning, the retired carpenter drove up and down alleys collecting things people threw away. "Junking" he called it. He always came by early because, he said, "This old robin is the early bird that catches the worms." Back home in his workshop, he'd clean what needed cleaning and fix what needed fixing. Then he'd sell it all at Greenfield's flea market.

His truck creaked to a stop at the Aldens' fence. "Mornin'," he called.

The children waved. "Good morning, Mr. Robbins," said Violet.

"And why, may I ask, are the Alden children up and out so early in the day?"

"We're having a yard sale," said Benny. "Do you think people will buy our things?"

Mr. Robbins laughed. "Benny, my boy, one man's trash is another man's treasure. Just because you're done with a thing doesn't mean someone else can't make good use of it. Good luck," he said, his truck rattling off down the alley.

Henry finished sanding his cashier table and set it on top of two sawhorses he had found in the garage. Next, he set out their money box, which was really an old fishing-tackle box that Grandfather said they could use for the sale. Yesterday, Henry had cleaned out all of the rusty hooks, broken bobbers, and dried-up rubber worms, then gave the box a good scrubbing. Now he made a sign for his table:

$$ CASHIER, PLEASE PAY HERE $$

"I'm ready," he said.

"Me, too," said Violet.

"Me, three," said Benny.

What they needed now were customers.

*****

Their yard-sale signs worked! All day long, people strolled through the Aldens' backyard. A few came just to see the famous old boxcar that stood next to the fountain in the garden. But nearly everyone bought at least one thing. And Violet's lemonade and cookies were selling fast!

By four o'clock, the last few shoppers had left the yard. Henry's tackle box was crammed with coins and bills. He looked at his watch. "Time to stop for today," he said.

Benny frowned at the nearly empty tables. "We hardly have anything left!"

"That's great," said Henry. "We want to sell our old stuff to make money to buy something new."

Benny still looked unhappy. "But our signs say the sale is Saturday and Sunday. What will we sell tomorrow?"

"Wait," said Violet, running into the house. She came back lugging a shopping bag filled with her *Prairie Girls* adventure books. "I've read these so many times, I know them by heart." Now that she'd turned ten, she was ready to read something new. Benny helped her put the books on a table.

"I'll go collect the signs," said Jessie, "so they won't be ruined if it rains tonight." She wheeled the wagon out of the yard.

Henry unstuffed the money from the box and made piles of one-, five-, and twenty-dollar bills. Next, he sorted the pennies, nickels, dimes, and quarters into the tackle box compartments.

"How much did we make?" asked Benny.

"I don't know yet," Henry said. "We'll count it together when Jessie comes home. Meanwhile, we can clean up."

A skinny woman wearing a floppy hat wandered into the yard. Her big sunglasses made her look like an owl. The cart she pushed overflowed with old silverware, teapots, dolls, and lace. Clearly, she had been to many other sales that day.

"Sorry," Henry said, "but we're closed. Please come back tomorrow."

"I'm just looking," she snapped, wheeling her cart from table to table. "Just looking."

Violet wiped the lemonade table with damp paper towels, then packed the leftover cookies into plastic bags to sell the next day.

"What can I do?" asked Benny.

"You can bring me the boxcar donations," said Henry.

Benny ran back to the old railroad car. A poster set against a tree stump said:

Tour a real boxcar, $1.
All tour money will be donated to the
Greenfield Homeless Shelter.

A large metal Crispy Crackers can sat on the stump near the sign. When the Alden children lived in the boxcar, they heated their water in this can. Now, instead of water, the old green can was filled with dollar bills.

Benny brought it to Henry.

"Great," said Henry. "We'll count this later, too." He pressed the lid on the can. It was so rusty he had to pound it with his fist to make it stay shut. He set the can under his table while he finished sorting the yard sale money.

The woman with the floppy hat wheeled her cart toward Henry. "Nothing here for me," she said. "I'm looking for old things, antiques." She peered over the tops of her glasses at the tackle box. "How much do you want for that?"

"This?" said Henry. "It's not for sale."

"Humph," she said. "Figures." She jutted her chin toward Violet's books. "How much?"

"Ah-um…" *What was the right price?* She didn't know. "Ah-um, twenty-five cents each?" Had she asked too much for such old books? The woman grabbed all the *Prairie Girl* books from the table and shoved them into her cart. She threw down a few dollar bills and hurried off.

Jessie pulled the wagon full of signs into the yard. She shook her head at all the bare tables. "We're going to need a lot more things to sell tomorrow."

Violet sighed. All she had left were a few barrettes and two dolls with no clothes. "I brought out everything I could find."

"Me, too," said Jessie.

Henry put the bills into the tackle box and snapped the latches shut. "Well," he said, with a sly grin, "I guess I could sell my old hockey skates."

"You wouldn't!" said Benny, who was waiting to grow big enough to wear them.

"Henry," Violet said, "don't tease."

Henry smiled. "Oh, all right. Then I guess I don't have anything, either."

Violet picked up the pitcher of lemonade to take inside. "We should ask Grandfather if he has things we can sell."

A moving truck rumbled down the street and screeched to a stop at the Aldens' driveway. "Best Movers" was painted on the side. Violet thought the truck needed a good washing. She guessed someone else did, too, because *Wash Me* was written in the dust on the side of the truck.

"Hey," called the driver, waving a piece of paper, "any of you kids know where..." he squinted at the paper, "....where..." he squinted harder, "where I can find 332 Locust?"

"Sure," said Henry, pointing. "That's two blocks over and one block down."

"Thanks." The driver squinted at Violet's pitcher. "Is that lemonade?"

"Ice cold," said Henry. "Twenty-five cents a cup."

"I'll take two," said the driver. "Driving this rig is thirsty work. Can't wait to drive up to Minnesota where it's nice and cool."

Violet poured the lemonade. The driver chugged the first cupful without taking even one breath.

"Are new people moving in on Locust?" asked Jessie, hoping for another twelve-year-old girl to play with.

"Nope," said the driver, "moving out, to

Minneapolis." He finished the second cup as quickly as the first. "Boy, that sure hit the spot. Thanks." He handed Violet a dollar. "Keep the change."

Benny watched the truck drive away. He seemed deep in thought. Suddenly, he turned to the others. "We've got to get over there," he said.

"Where?" asked Henry.

"332 Locust."

"Why?"

"Because, when people move, they throw out all kinds of great stuff. Stuff they don't want to take with them."

"So?" asked Violet.

"Maybe we'll find things to sell at our yard sale!"

"Good thinking," said Henry. "I'll come with you, but first we need to put all of our things inside the garage in case it rains again."

"I'll bring the wagon with us to Locust Street," said Jessie as she unloaded her signs.

The children quickly brought the few

items they hadn't sold into the garage and began to walk towards Locust.

Violet lagged behind. Warning shivers tickled her spine. Some of those big old houses on Locust looked creepy.

Jessie stopped at the corner and looked back. "Violet," she called, waving, "hurry up."

"C-c-coming," said Violet, running after them, wondering just what sort of things they would find.

CHAPTER 2

A Wooden Mask

Five minutes later, the children stood in front of 332 Locust. Faded blue paint chipped and peeled off the old house. Thick weeds choked the flowerbeds and grew up through cracks in the walk. Hot summers and freezing winters had turned the white picket fence a dirty gray. A few broken pickets poked jagged edges in all directions. Violet backed away. "Let's go home," she said.

"Wait," said Jessie. "I know this house. We trick-or-treated here. Remember? The housekeeper was that funny lady dressed as a mummy. She brought us into the living room—"

"To a nice old lady in a wheelchair," said Violet. "I *do* remember. She was dressed like Betsy Ross and was sewing an American flag."

"I don't remember," Benny said.

"Sure you do," said Jessie. "There was a big silver candleholder on the table next to her with five black-and-orange candles. Candle wax was dripping onto the table, and you picked up a glob and shaped it into a ball."

Benny's eyes grew wide. "And she let me ride up and down the staircase in her special elevator."

"This house was so cluttered with all of her things," Henry said, "that I wondered how her wheelchair got through. No wonder they need such a big moving truck."

Jessie remembered the stacks of books,

piles of pictures, and shelves of figurines that were scattered through the big blue house.

The children looked around. A red car, as bright and shiny as a candy apple, was parked in front of 332 Locust, but no Best Movers truck. "Where is it?" asked Violet.

"Maybe the driver stopped for gas," said Jessie.

"Or dinner," said Benny, who was usually hungry. "Let's go see what they're throwing away."

The children ran around the block and looked down the alley. "Oh, no!" cried Benny.

Empty trash cans stood neatly next to garages. At the far end of the alley, a Greenfield garbage truck rattled away. Two workers walked behind the truck, picking up trash cans, bags, and boxes, emptying everything into the truck. One man pulled a lever. A loud whirring and grinding noise filled the air as the truck crushed everything inside.

"We're too late," said Violet.

Benny watched the garbage truck turn down the next alley. He felt sad as he thought about all of the treasures they could have found.

"That's too bad," said Jessie. "It was a great idea."

Henry put an arm around his brother. "Cheer up," he said. "Let's go home and open the tackle box, see how much we made today."

Usually, Benny liked counting money. But now he lagged behind the others, kicking pebbles as he walked. At the end of the alley, as he turned to kick one last stone, he saw a woman with long red hair wedge a large white box into a trash can behind the blue house. She leaned out into the alley, staring at the distant garbage truck, then hurried back inside the house.

Benny raced over and lifted the lid.

"What did you find?" asked Henry.

Benny pulled out the box and opened it. Popcorn spilled out. "Popcorn?" he said. "Why throw away popcorn?"

"Sometimes," said Violet, "people pack fragile things in popcorn."

"Fragile?" asked Benny.

"Fragile means things that can break easily. Like the glass snow globes Grandfather sent from New York. Those were packed in popcorn to keep them from breaking. Popcorn's cheaper than bubble wrap."

"And it tastes better," said Benny.

"You should never eat packing corn," warned Violet. "It can be months and months old and dirty."

The others bent over and looked into the box as Jessie slowly uncovered their new treasure. "It looks like some kind of mask or something," she said.

The children all stared at the wooden mask that lay neatly in the box. The colors were faded, and a crown of dusty feathers sprouted from the top and sides. The face was half faded yellow and half gray, and the bottom of the mask was painted in different colors, almost like a rainbow. On both sides of the face, rain clouds had been painted.

"Wow!" said Benny. "Look at how thick these feathers are!" He ran his fingers from

the bottom to the top of each bunch of feathers.

Violet looked carefully at the mask before speaking. "I read about something like this in one of my *Prairie Girls* books," she said. "It looks like the face of one of the dolls that Katrina found in the book *Katrina and the Kachina Doll*."

"That's right," said Jessie. "My teacher talked about kachinas at school. Kachinas are Native American spirits. The tribes made dolls of the spirits to give to women and children as presents. But I've never heard of anything like this."

"I wonder what it was used for," Henry said.

"Do you think it's real?" asked Benny, very excited.

Henry began to close the box. "I'm sure this is just a copy of a Native American mask. Maybe the person who lives here bought it as a souvenir and didn't want it anymore."

"I'm going to sell it tomorrow," Benny

decided. "I bet someone pays five dollars for it."

Violet looked at the mask carefully before Henry closed the lid all the way. "This must be a copy. But why would someone pack it so nicely just to throw it in the trash?"

Everyone nodded in agreement.

"Let's stop at the library on the way home. They might have some books on kachinas," said Henry.

As they wheeled the wagon out of the alley, an orange pickup truck pulled in. The children moved aside as it passed. The man driving was skinny with a scruffy black beard. He glanced at the children as he drove by, and seemed puzzled when he saw their wagon with the box inside. As he drove off down the alley, the children saw parts of an old swing set and a couple of broken bikes in the back of his truck.

Benny laughed. "He's probably a junker trying to catch up to the garbage truck. But I'll bet Mr. Robbins already picked up all the good stuff."

*****

The head librarian typed "kachina" into her computer. "Ah, here we go," said Ms. Connelly, printing out a list of titles. "These will get you started."

The library lights flashed on and off. "Oh, no," Jessie said, "the library's closing."

"We still have fifteen minutes," said Violet, running toward the computer room. "I'll see what information I can find online."

As Violet headed toward the computer room, Henry, Jessie, and Benny quickly found the books from the list the librarian had given them.

"My book says that kachinas are spirits from the Hopi Native American tribe that live in Arizona," said Jessie. "It says there are many different kinds of kachinas."

"My book says that a few Native American tribes have kachina spirits, but the Hopi tribe has the most," Henry noted. "The Hopi dress up as kachinas by wearing masks like the one we found. The masks are very special to them. When the Hopi tribe wears these masks in their ceremonies, they believe they become the kachina spirits," Henry explained.

"What kind of spirits are they?" Benny asked. "Are they like ghosts?"

"No Benny," said Henry. "The Hopi spirits help give the tribe the things they need to survive. Each spirit is responsible for something important to the Hopi tribe."

"Like food?" asked Benny.

"Yes, Benny," Henry answered with a laugh. Benny loved to eat. "But there are also kachinas that control the weather and the earth."

"There are also clown kachinas that are there just for fun," chimed in Jessie.

"And scary kachinas that are used to frighten children into being good," said Henry, tickling Benny.

*****

In the computer room, Violet paced up and down. Every computer was taken. *Someone please leave*, she thought, *please, please, please*. Finally, a man with a long braid down his back stood and pushed back his chair. He reached out to turn off his computer. Violet froze. He wore a beautiful bracelet decorated with dark and light silver. It was just like a Hopi bracelet she had seen in her book. She glanced at his computer screen. It was filled with photographs of old masks. *Could they be kachina masks?* The screen went blue as he logged off.

The library lights flashed again. Violet didn't have time to go online so she hurried to find the others. Jessie was flipping through a book of kachina masks while Henry read a book to Benny.

Jessie quickly looked up from her book. "Look!"

"What is it, Jessie?" asked Violet.

"This mask looks a lot like ours. It's very dark on one side, light on the other, and there's the same colorful chin. It says here this mask represents a Hopi cloud kachina maiden." Jessie continued. "The cloud kachinas bring rain to the tribe, and make their crops grow."

"I think someone copied our mask from

one of these books, the way I copy drawings and paintings from Grandfather's old art books," said Violet.

"Isn't that cheating?" asked Benny as Henry grabbed their pile of books to check out.

"Artists copy other people's art all the time. It's a good way to learn."

"I bet it's still worth something," Benny said. "I bet I can sell it tomorrow for more than five dollars!"

CHAPTER 3

Missing!

The dinner table buzzed with excited voices as the children told Grandfather about the yard sale and the old blue house and the mask Benny found.

"Wait, I'll show you!" Benny dashed to his room and brought back the mask. "Look," he said.

"Grandfather," said Violet. "We don't have much left to sell tomorrow. Could you donate a few old things for our yard sale?"

"Hmmm," Grandfather tried to think. "I'm not sure I..."

"You most certainly do," said Mrs. McGregor, the housekeeper, whisking in from the kitchen.

Grandfather looked puzzled. "I do?"

Mrs. McGregor set down a fresh-baked orange cake and bowl of strawberries. "All that clutter in the garage. It's been years since those shelves had a good cleaning!" She sliced cake for the children and piled strawberries on top. "I'd do it myself, except it's not for me to decide what needs keeping and what needs throwing away." She cut a nice big slice for Grandfather and slid it in front of him. "I always say that many hands make light work. The five of you could clean that garage in no time, and the children might find things for their sale."

Grandfather looked around the table at the children's hopeful faces. "Well," he said, smiling as he lifted a forkful of cake, "we'd better finish eating as fast as we can. It seems we have a great deal of work to do."

*****

What riches awaited them in the big old garage! Grandfather climbed a ladder, passing down rusty golf clubs, typewriters, paintings, dishes, garden tools, skis for snow and water, tools, and model airplane kits. They cleared shelf after shelf, filling their yard-sale tables with things they could sell, throwing the rest into garbage bags.

When they finally finished, Henry lugged the heavy bags to the alley. The orange pickup truck he'd seen on Locust rolled by. Henry noticed the truck still had the same swing set and bicycles in the back as the day before. The pickup slowed to a stop. Henry thought the driver's black beard looked as scruffy as Watch's coat did before a bath.

The driver stared at Henry. "Hey," he said, "aren't you one of the kids I saw in the alley over at—"

"Henry!" Grandfather called from the garage.

The driver's head jerked up as if he were surprised someone else was around.

"I'm in the alley," Henry called back.

Grandfather rounded the corner carrying an armful of fishing poles as the orange truck sped off.

*****

The second day of the sale was even busier than the first. From early morning, people crowded the yard, buying everything in sight. At first, Benny set the mask on his table between Grandfather's postcard collection and a shoebox full of plastic dinosaurs. But, every time someone came to look at the mask, Benny's stomach felt all fluttery. *Don't buy it, don't buy it, don't buy it,* he'd think.

The truth was, he couldn't bear to sell it—not for five dollars, or fifty dollars, or a hundred million "bajillion" dollars. He wanted to keep it for his very own—forever. Benny put the mask in its white box and hid it under an old blanket on a shelf in the garage.

Mr. Robbins came by, stopping at Henry's cashier table. "Just checking to see how you're doing," he said. "Looks like the Alden children run a mighty fine sale."

"It's a lot of work," said Henry, "but it's also a lot of fun."

The orange pickup pulled to a stop in front of the house, and the driver climbed out.

"That's the man I saw over on Locust," said Benny, "the day we found the mask."

"I saw him last night," Henry said, "while we were cleaning out the garage."

The man walked into the yard, quickly moving from table to table as if looking for something in particular. Henry pointed out the man to Mr. Robbins. "He's been driving through the alleys," said Henry. "Do you know him?"

Mr. Robbins studied the man. "Can't say I do. I guess he's not an early bird, like me. I've never seen him selling at the flea market, either. Must be new around here. Well, I think I'll go treat myself to some of your sister's lemonade and a cookie or two."

The floppy-hat lady wheeled her shopping cart into the yard. Once again it overflowed with yard-sale items. She peered over the tops of her owlish glasses. "You have new things, I see. These look much more interesting."

Jessie watched as the woman brushed her hand across a few items on one of their tables and marched straight into the garage. Jessie followed her and found her thumbing through their neatly stacked boxes.

Jessie walked over to the woman and politely tapped her on the shoulder, "Excuse me."

The woman jumped, surprised to see Jessie standing next to her.

"Only the things on the tables are for sale," Jessie told her.

"Humph," the woman said as she quickly walked away from Jessie towards the boxcar.

Violet was so busy pouring lemonade and selling cookies that she didn't notice a man approach.

"I'd like a lemonade, please," said a strong voice. She looked up, right into the eyes of the man with the braid she'd seen at the library computer. He was wearing the same silver bracelet with the dark and light silver decorations.

"That's a beautiful bracelet," said Violet, handing him his drink. "Is it Hopi?"

The man's eyebrows shot up. "And how would you know that?"

"From my *Prairie Girls* books. The Hopis are famous for making jewelry that has light silver on top of dark silver. It's called…it's called…," she tried to remember.

"Overlay," he said. "Silver overlay. And, yes, this is Hopi." He sipped his lemonade thoughtfully. "Do you have any Hopi items for sale?"

"Oh, no, mostly just stuff from the garage. Although, my brother found an old mask yesterday that looks a lot like a kachina mask. Probably an old souvenir." Violet glanced at Benny's table, but the mask was gone. "I guess he sold it," she said. "Sorry."

"Hey," a little boy tugged Violet's shirt and held up a quarter. "Can I have a cookie?"

Violet looked down at the empty cookie platter. "Oops, I'll bring some right out."

She ran to the house, pulling open the screen door.

That was the exact moment the neighbor's cat decided to prance through their yard. Watch dashed out the screen door before Violet could stop him. The cat ran, Watch chased, the cat screeched, Watch barked. They ran in and out, over and under, upsetting tables, knocking over baskets.

"Stop," shouted Henry, trying to catch them. "Watch, stop!" Finally, Jessie ran one way and Henry ran the other until, together, they trapped Watch. "You're grounded," said Henry, grabbing Watch's collar and pulling him into the house. "I'll let you out when the sale is over."

At day's end, Benny flopped down on the grass, too tired to move. Grandfather came out of the house. "I just received word that a friend in Florida needs my help. I need to fly there late tonight. But I had planned a surprise to thank you for helping me clean out the garage." He glanced at his watch. "If we hurry, we'll get there with just enough time for hamburgers and a round of miniature golf. That is," he smiled at Benny, "if you're not too tired."

"Miniature golf!" Benny jumped up. His second favorite thing in the world, after eating, was playing miniature golf. As it happened, they had time for two games of golf. Benny made the hardest shot of the day— hitting his golf ball through a turning windmill and under a bridge—on his very first try.

By the time Grandfather pulled up in front of their house, night stars filled the sky. "I'll be home in a couple of days," he said. "Take care of Mrs. McGregor." And he waved as he drove off.

The weary children walked up the driveway. "Hey," said Henry, "it looks like the garage door's open. Did anyone lock it?"

None of them had.

"Let me get my mask," said Benny, running inside. "Oh, no" he cried. It looked as if a tornado had ripped through the garage— boxes tipped over, old clothing thrown all around.

Jessie stared, wide-eyed. "Who would do this?"

"We just cleaned this garage," said Violet.

"My mask," wailed Benny, digging through the rubble. "My mask! Somebody stole my mask."

"It must be here," said Henry. The children searched and searched, but the mask was gone.

"What else did they steal?" Jessie asked.

"Our money!" Henry clambered through the clutter to the workbench, digging through a pile of old clothes. "Here!" he said as he lifted the tackle box, quickly opening the latches. All their money was still stacked neatly inside. "Whew," he said. "It's a good thing the thief didn't see this."

"What about the homeless shelter donations?" cried Jessie, running to the boxcar.

The tree stump was empty. The thief had stolen the green Crispy Cracker can. "How *could* they?" she said.

"Look!" said Benny. Moonlight shone on a trail of white popcorn. The children followed it from the garage to the alley, where it suddenly stopped.

"It looks like the thief carried the box with the mask this far," said Henry, "then climbed into a car."

A sudden gust of wind stirred scraps of white cardboard that were scattered around the alley. Benny picked one up. "This is the box the mask was in." They searched all around, finding more scraps and a few popcorn crumbs, but no mask.

Henry thought about the man in the orange truck. The man had seen them in the alley on Locust where they'd found the mask. Then he'd come by last night when they were cleaning the garage. And he was at the yard sale today. Could he have known they had the mask and come to steal it?

"What if our mask wasn't a copy?" said Henry, "What if it was a *real* kachina mask like the ones we saw in the library book?"

"I think I saw a man looking at kachina masks online when we were at the library," said Violet. She told them about the man with the braid who wore a Hopi bracelet. He had been at the library, and he had also come to their yard sale. "He asked if we had any Hopi things for sale. Maybe he knew about the mask. Maybe he came back to steal it."

"And don't forget the lady with the big glasses and floppy hat," said Jessie. "She was only interested in old things. And I saw her going through boxes of stuff in the garage. Maybe she saw the mask and knew it was valuable. Maybe she came back to take it."

This time, the children locked the garage door good and tight before going into the house. One thing was for sure, a thief had come while they were away, a thief who thought their mask was worth stealing. Now the children had to find out why. It was just the sort of mystery the Alden children loved.

CHAPTER 4

Popcorn Whiskers

"It's all my fault." A sorrowful Mrs. McGregor sat on the sofa. "I let Watch out in the yard for a bit of exercise while I relaxed inside. I *did* hear him barking. But he'd been barking all day, what with so many strangers coming and going. And, well, I just thought he was barking at some old squirrel. I mean, any other time I would have gone out and checked. But," she looked sadder than ever, "I was watching "What a Wacky

World." It was, the children knew, her favorite TV show. "And tonight was the final contest to see who would be voted the wackiest. By the time I went to check on Watch, he'd gotten out."

"He can't get out of the yard by himself," said Henry.

Mrs. McGregor shrugged. "All I know is, I found Watch in the alley. He was chewing on a box and looking very pleased with himself."

"Was there a mask in the box?" asked Benny.

"Mask? No, nothing like that. Just bits of chewed cardboard. And popcorn. Oh, Watch was having a regular picnic. I had to drag him back into the yard and brush popcorn crumbs from his whiskers."

"Maybe he ate the mask, too," said Benny. The children looked at Watch. Watch looked at the children, tilting his head to one side. Benny knew that even Watch couldn't eat a wooden mask.

"Was the garage door open?" asked Jessie.

"I didn't notice," Mrs. McGregor said. "I was so upset about Watch getting out of the yard that all I thought about was getting him home and cleaning him up."

Jessie patted Mrs. McGregor's shoulder. "It's all right," she said. "We're all to blame. We were so excited about going to miniature golf that we forgot to lock the garage."

"Do you think," Violet said softly, "we should call the police?"

Mrs. McGregor scrunched her brow, thinking. "Perhaps," she said, "you should call your grandfather's friend Tom Morgan. He's a retired policeman with a good head and a good heart. He'll know what to do."

*****

Officer Morgan didn't give the children much hope. "It sounds like there's not much we can do," he said. Henry put the call on speaker phone so all the children could listen at once. "The garage door was left open, so anyone could have walked in. And you left a can of money on a tree stump, anyone could have walked off with that as well."

"Can't you find my mask?" asked Benny.

Officer Morgan was quiet a moment. "I don't expect we'll find many clues," he said. "But I'll send a policeman over to take a look around and file a report. I'd come myself except I'm helping friends over at Pleasant Valley Park. But I promise I'll stop by tomorrow."

Henry hung up the phone. "I'm not sure Officer Morgan is right," he said. "We do have one clue. Whoever broke into the garage left the tackle box full of money behind."

"Why would they do that?" asked Benny.

"Maybe they didn't come looking for money. Maybe they came looking for the mask."

Jessie looked puzzled. "If you're right, and they didn't come to steal money, why did they take the Crispy Crackers can with the homeless shelter donations?"

They all fell silent, thinking. But none of them could think of an answer. Finally, Henry said, "We need to go back where this all began. We need to go back to 332 Locust and look for more clues."

"That house will be empty," said Violet, who still thought the old house looked creepy. "The man with the moving truck said the people were moving to Minnesota."

Henry nodded. "Let's just bike over and take a look around. At least we'll be doing *something*."

Jessie tried to cheer them up by setting out a plate of leftover cookies. Henry poured everyone a glass of milk. The snack did help them feel a little better.

Still, after they went to bed, it was a long time before anyone fell asleep.

CHAPTER 5

A History Mystery

The next morning, as the children pulled their bikes in front of the old blue house, they saw a young man in a robe and pajamas stomping around in the bushes. "May I help you?" he asked.

"Did you just move in?" asked Jessie.

"Me? Oh, dear me, no. I'm visiting from California. My grandmother lives here."

"The nice lady in the wheelchair?" Jessie asked.

"The very same. Ah!" he dove into the bushes and came out clutching a soggy copy of the *Greenfield Gazette*. "The newspaper boy has a terrible throwing arm."

"We'd like to talk to your grandmother," said Henry. "Is she home?"

"Of course she is. The poor dear took an awful spill and broke her hip. She still needs a lot of rest.

"Lyle, dear," called a voice from the house. "Have you found the *Gazette?*"

"I have," he said. He smiled at the children. "Please come in and say hello. My grandmother absolutely adores company."

The living room looked totally different than when the children had trick-or-treated. Gone was the clutter of furniture and knick-knacks. All that was left were a few tables, a couple of chairs, a wheelchair folded in the corner, and a large bed. A cheerful woman with curly white hair sat propped up on a mountain of pillows. "Why," she said, smiling brightly, "who have we here?" The children introduced themselves.

"Call me Grandma Belle," she said. "Everybody does. I wish I had cookies to give you. My old nurse baked all the time, but my new nurse, Nurse Rumple, doesn't bake at all." She winked. "I'll make certain to have treats for your next visit. Please sit a moment."

"May I ride your wheelchair?" asked Benny.

Grandma Belle laughed. "Why, of course." And with that, Benny hopped into the chair and began wheeling around the large room.

"Did the moving van take away all your furniture?" asked Henry.

"Moving van? Heavens, no. Whatever gave you that idea?"

He told her about the Best Movers driver who was looking for 332 Locust. "If you're not moving," said Henry, "where are all your things?"

"Well, when I broke my hip and couldn't get around very well, I had them bring my bed down to this nice bright living room. When I hired Nurse Rumple, she couldn't stand all my clutter. She said, "It's not healthy to live among dusty old things," and she moved most everything out to the garage. I must admit, it is much neater this way." She looked around the room. "But to tell the truth, I miss having all my things around."

"I think the house looks nice and bright," said Violet.

"And clean," said Grandma Belle. "These past few days, Nurse Rumple has been scrubbing, scrubbing, scrubbing, washing furniture and fixtures, floors and doors. She's even been wearing rubber gloves to keep from making smudges. She said she wants to leave everything spic and span when the new nurse comes tomorrow."

"Is that why she threw that old mask away?" asked Benny, turning the wheelchair around and around in circles.

"Mask? What mask?"

Benny told her about the mask in the box.

"I'm sure I had something of the sort at one time or another, but with everything packed away, there's nothing to jog my memory," said Grandma Belle.

She took off her eyeglasses, wiping them slowly with a tissue. "If it's the mask I'm thinking of, it's one of the ones my father gave me when I was a little girl. He gave me lots of things he had found in the Arizona desert when he was a boy. That's where he grew up, you see. He and his friends came across the most interesting things—rattlesnake skeletons and animal skulls, kachina dolls and pots made from desert clay."

"Do you still have them?" asked Benny.

"They're all around here somewhere, I imagine. My father never could bear to get rid of any of his things. Nor could I. But these past few years it's become hard for me to care for everything. Hard to wheel my chair around this house with all my things lying around. I have managed to give a few things away to friends, but I could never part with all of it."

She lay back on the pillows. "Nurse Rumple is at the grocery store just now," she said, "but I'll be sure to ask her about the mask the moment she returns. I certainly hope she hasn't mixed my precious things in with the garbage. And you must promise to come visit again soon."

"We will," said the children. And they left Grandma Belle to her morning nap.

*****

As they began to walk home, a Best Movers truck rumbled past them. *Wash me* was written in the dust on the side. "That's the same van that stopped and asked us for directions," said Henry. "The driver said he was looking for 332 Locust. But Grandma Belle isn't moving."

"And he said he was going to drive to Minnesota," said Jessie. "So why is he still here in Greenfield?"

"I'll bet he's not a mover at all," said Benny. "I'll bet he's a thief who just drives around, looking for people to rob."

Henry whistled softly. "No one would suspect a moving truck driver taking things out of a house."

"Do you think he robbed us?" asked Violet.

"Come on," said Henry, "let's follow him." The four young detectives pedaled their hardest, trying to keep the truck in view. A few blocks later, it pulled up to a house on Locust. The children stopped their bikes across the street and quickly hid behind a parked car, watching the driver climb out of the truck to ring the doorbell. After a while, he rang again. When there was no answer, he walked around to the back.

"He's seeing if anyone's home," Jessie said. A minute later, the front door opened. "Oh!" She gasped as the driver walked out of the house carrying a TV set. "He must have broken into the back!"

The man put the TV in his truck, then went back in the house. "Let's get the police," said Violet.

"Hold on," Henry said, watching as the man wheeled out a large chair and a computer, then went back inside. "I'm going to take a quick look inside his truck. If he left the

keys, I can grab them so he can't drive away."

Henry's heart thumped like a drum as he raced across the street. He had to hurry before the driver saw him. Quickly, he climbed up on the truck's running board. Next to the driver's seat was a map of Greenfield and a pair of broken eyeglasses. One lens was missing, and the other was badly cracked. Henry saw a clipboard on the driver's seat with a work order for a moving job on Locust. As he read the piece of paper, he started to smile. He jumped off the truck and ran back across the street. "I think I know what hap—"

"Hey!" shouted the driver, barreling out of the house towards them, "Hey!"

"Oh, no," cried Benny. "Let's get out of here!"

"It's all right," said Henry.

"But—"

The driver rushed up and squinted at them. "Aren't you the lemonade kids?" He broke into a wide smile. "Best danged lemonade I ever tasted. Told my wife about it.

She said I should ask for your recipe."

Benny stepped forward to speak. "Why did you tell us you were moving Grandma Belle?"

"Grandma who?"

Henry put his hands on Benny's shoulders. "It's all right." He turned to the driver. "When you stopped at our house that day to ask us directions, you thought you were looking for 332 Locust, didn't you?"

"Yup."

"But you were really looking for..." Henry pointed to the numbers on the house across the street, "882."

The man nodded. "Broke my specs the other day." He looked embarrassed. "Sat on 'em by mistake. I can drive okay without glasses, but when I try reading things up close like that work order, everything's a little blurry. Those eights sure looked like threes to me. I was a whole five blocks off."

Violet jotted down her recipe, which was one can of frozen lemonade and three cans of water mixed with the juice of a fresh-squeezed lemon. "And my secret trick," she said, "is to make extra lemonade a day ahead of time and freeze it in ice cube trays. Using lemonade ice cubes keeps lemonade from getting watery."

"Thanks," said the driver, tucking the recipe into his pocket. "Well, better get back to work."

The children climbed on their bikes. "I'm hungry," said Benny.

Henry checked his watch. It was eleven-thirty. "I guess we might as well eat before we go to the library."

"All right!" said Benny, pedaling faster than everyone all the way to the Greenfield Diner.

CHAPTER 6

Henry's List

As they wheeled their bikes into the diner's bike rack, an orange pickup truck came speeding down the street. "Isn't that the same—" Jessie began, just as the truck squealed around in a U-turn.

"He is one very bad driver," said Henry. The truck screeched to a stop behind a bright red car parked in front of Ye Olde Antique Shoppe. "He nearly hit that car!"

A woman with long red hair ran out of the

shop and started yelling at the driver. "She sure looks angry," said Violet. "Maybe that's her car he nearly hit."

Benny stared. "I think that's Grandma Belle's nurse."

"Are you sure?"

He looked hard, trying to remember. "She's the woman I saw put the mask in the garbage can. I remember her long red hair."

The angry woman's voice grew louder. A few of her words drifted across the street. "...do you mean...you can't...find it?...has to be..."

"Benny's right," said Henry, locking his bike. "The car she just got out of is the same car we saw in front of Grandma Belle's."

Jessie pursed her lips. "But Grandma Belle said her nurse was at the grocery store. That's all the way across town."

"Maybe she likes antiques," said Violet, who very much loved old things.

"...where else..." came the woman's voice, "...could it....Find it!"

"It sounds like they know each other," said

Jessie. Suddenly, the woman climbed into the little red car and sped away.

The driver of the orange truck squealed another U-turn. The broken swing set and bikes in the back of the truck nearly flew out.

Inside the diner, the children found a table near the big front window and gave the waitress their orders—chicken fingers for Violet, a hamburger for Henry, grilled cheese for Jessie, and a hot dog for Benny. Waiting for food to come was always the hardest part.

The smell of hamburgers sizzling on the grill made the children's stomachs growl. Benny moved the ketchup bottle in front of him so he'd be ready to squirt ketchup on his plate the second his food came. Usually they played games of tic-tac-toe or dot-to-dot to take their minds off how hungry they were. But today, Henry opened a paper napkin and took out a pencil.

"What are you doing?" Jessie asked.

"Trying to figure out who could have stolen Benny's mask and taken the Crispy Crackers can full of money." Henry knew that making lists helped him think. On the top of the napkin he wrote: SUSPECTS.

The others crowded around, watching. Under SUSPECTS, Henry wrote:

Driver of orange truck

> *In alley behind Grandma Belle's the day we found the mask.*

> *In our alley the night we cleaned the garage.*

> *At our yard sale.*

> *In town with Grandma Belle's nurse.*

"What about the lady with the floppy hat and big sunglasses?" asked Benny. "Jessie said she was looking through the shelves in the garage. That's where I hid my mask. Maybe she saw it and decided to come back later to steal it so she wouldn't have to pay for it." Henry wrote:

Lady in floppy hat

> *At yard sale both days.*

> *Only wanted to buy old things.*

> *Jessie saw her going through boxes in the garage.*

"Anyone else?" Henry asked.

"What about the man at the library?" asked Violet. "The one with the silver bracelet? I thought I saw a kachina mask on his computer screen. And the next day he came to our yard sale asking if we had any Hopi things for sale."

Henry added:

Man with braid

 At library—looking at Hopi masks?

 At yard sale—wanted Hopi things.

"What about the nurse?" asked Henry. "She could have accidentally thrown the mask away, but what if it wasn't an accident? What if she was trying to steal it?"

"She isn't where she told Grandma Belle she would be," added Jessie.

"And we just saw her talking to the man in the orange truck," said Violet.

Henry scribbled:

Grandma Belle's nurse

 Accidentally threw away mask?

 Seen with the man in the orange truck.

"We have a lot of questions with no answers," said Henry, as their food arrived.

"Maybe we should go back to the library and find out more about these masks," said Jessie. "If someone wants our mask bad enough to steal it, it has to be worth something."

And with that the children turned all their attention to eating.

*****

After lunch, they rode to the library. A large poster on the library door said:
Intertribal Powwow
Saturday-Sunday—Pleasant Valley Park.
Native American dancing, singing,
drumming, crafts, food.
Everyone welcome.

"What's a powwow?" asked Benny.

"It's a big gathering of Native Americans," Violet explained. "Like a big party where there's music and dancing and storytelling."

"And cake?"

"Well, maybe not cake, But there are many other treats served. I read about powwows in one of my *Prairie Girls* books, *Katrina and the Kachina Doll*. Katrina was invited to a powwow. She learned to make jewelry out of porcupine quills and to stitch moccasins out of buffalo hide."

Violet sat at a computer and typed in "kachina masks." Henry found a Hopi kachina book with the photographs of masks.

"This web site has old kachina masks for sale," said Violet. "All of the antique masks are sold for…" Her eyes grew wide as she stared at the screen.

"What?" said Jessie. "Sold for what?"

"For thousands of dollars!" Violet scrolled down the screen until she came to a mask that looked like theirs. She read quietly a moment before printing the page she was reading.

"That's why someone wanted my mask so much!" said Benny.

"Grandma Belle said her father lived in Arizona," Jessie said. "She said he dug up things like this when he was a boy. The mask that we found is probably one of the things that he dug out of the desert."

"Was Grandma Belle's father a thief?" Benny asked. "Would he have taken something that didn't belong to him?

"I don't know Benny," said Jessie.

Violet grabbed a stack of paper off the printer while Henry went to check out the books he found. "I found a few articles about stolen kachinas being sold on the Internet. We should show them to Grandma Belle. Maybe the pictures of the mask will help jog her memory."

As they walked out of the library, they passed the man with the braid reading at a table. He hunched over his books. Jessie peered over his shoulder, then poked Violet and pointed. The man was reading books about kachinas and Hopis. Did he steal their mask? Was he looking through the books to find out if it was valuable?

CHAPTER 7

A Two-Horned Mask

The children rang the bell but no one answered. They knocked on the door. Still nothing.

"Grandma Belle can't go out with a broken hip," said Violet.

Benny peered through the window. "Her wheelchair's gone! I left it right there in the corner."

"Maybe she was feeling better," said Jessie, "and her grandson took her for a walk."

"Maybe they're sitting in the yard," said Henry.

The children ran around back, but the only thing they found in the yard was a group of small birds chirping along the walk.

"Look," said Benny. The birds were feasting on pieces of popcorn. The children followed the trail along the walk out to the alley to the trash. They quickly opened the trash cans. Two were empty, but a white box stuck out of the third. "Another one!" said Benny.

Henry lifted it out and tore it open. Popcorn spilled out. Inside was a red, white, and blue mask with two horns on the top. The wood was old and cracked, and the feathers sticking out of the top smelled musty.

Violet ran her fingers over the wood. "It's beautiful. Why would Grandma Belle throw this away?"

"It's probably Nurse Rumple cleaning out more clutter," said Jessie. "We have to warn her not to throw anything else away until we find out if these masks are copies or real kachina masks."

"I'll keep this mask here and wait here for them to come back," said Henry. "You go home and call Grandma Belle. Leave a message on her phone asking her to call us."

After the three children sped away, Henry discovered old gardening tools in the yard and quickly set to work. He was one of those people who couldn't bear standing around doing nothing. The tools had rusted from being left outside. Still, they were good enough to clear weeds from the flowerbeds, prune overgrown trees, and trim the bushes around the porch. If Grandma Belle would let him, he would plant a wonderful vegetable garden and grow flowers that would bloom all summer long.

*****

"Who's that?" said Jessie as they neared their house. A strange car sat in their driveway, and a stranger leaned against the hood. With his white beard, round belly, and bright red suspenders he reminded Benny of Santa Claus. Watch ran to the man, carrying a stick in his mouth.

"Good dog," said the man, taking the stick and patting Watch's head. Then he threw the stick far down the block. "Fetch!" he called, laughing heartily as Watch ran after it.

"Hello," said the children.

The man turned and smiled. "Why, I would know you anywhere," he said. "You look just like Aldens. I'm Officer Tom Morgan. I talked to you on the phone last night about your garage break-in. Sorry to be so late getting to you. Been busy helping some friends set up tepees for next week's powwow. Let's have a look at the scene of the crime."

The children led him back to garage. But when they opened the door, everything was tidy once more. "There you are," called a cheerful Mrs. McGregor as she came out of the house. "Cleaning up was the least I could do." She turned to Officer Morgan. "Those children worked so hard on this garage. Then someone came and tore it apart. I felt just awful that I didn't listen when Watch tried to warn me that a thief was out here."

Mrs. McGregor was so proud of her work that no one had the heart to tell her the truth. Not only had she cleaned the scene of the crime, she also cleaned away any clues the thief might have left.

Officer Morgan looked around. "Anything missing besides the mask and the can full of money?"

"Not that we know," said Violet.

Violet took out the internet articles she had printed out. "This looks like the mask they stole. We thought ours was a copy, but now we think it may be a real kachina mask."

Officer Morgan looked at the pictures very carefully.

"We found another mask today," said Benny. "It has two horns. Henry has it at Grandma Belle's."

"Wait, I'll show you." Violet ran into the house and returned with colored pencils and paper. She quickly sketched the horned mask, coloring in the red, white, and blue.

"This is exactly what it looked like?" asked Officer Morgan.

"Yes," Violet said.

"Exactly!" said Jessie, who held up the drawing, very proud of her artistic sister.

"You know," said Officer Morgan, "if you keep practicing, you might make an excellent police artist one day," he said with a wink. "Perhaps I can arrange for you to watch one work," he offered.

"I would like that," Violet said.

Watch ran up with a stick in his mouth, staring as Officer Morgan got into his car and drove away. The children stared too. It seemed a little odd that he appeared to be more interested in some old masks than in a can full of stolen money.

"I bet he thinks the masks are real," said Benny. "What if they are? What if," he broke into a wide grin, "they are worth a lot of money!"

*****

Henry worked hard cleaning out the flowerbeds. Hidden under the weeds he found petunias and zinnias, marigolds and snapdragons, larkspurs, and many flowers he had never seen before. He felt sure that someone had once loved and tended this garden. He turned the sprinkler on the flowers to give them a good drink, then set to work cutting back the bushes. Two hours later, he sat to rest on the front porch and admired his handiwork. Now that he'd trimmed the bushes, the front porch could be seen from the street. Maybe now the paperboy would be able to throw the newspaper all the way onto the porch.

A cold glass of Violet's lemonade would sure taste good right now. But Henry had to make do with cold water from the garden hose. As he put the tools back near the garage, he saw the red car parked in the alley. Could the nurse have come home while he was working out in front? Maybe Grandma Belle was home as well.

Henry ran around and rang the bell. Then he knocked. No answer. He wrote a note asking Grandma Belle to please call the Aldens. "We found another mask today outside of your house," Henry wrote. "Please don't throw away any more masks until we talk to you."

As he slipped the note under the front door, he heard a noise inside. "Hello?" he called. "Anyone home?" No answer. He pressed his ear to the door and knocked. Nothing. He waited a long time but didn't hear anything more. He picked up the box with the two-horned mask and climbed on his bike. Shivers prickled the back of his neck. He whirled around. Did the front curtain move? Was someone there? He watched and waited, but the curtain—if it had indeed moved before—never moved again.

It's nothing, he thought, nothing at all. Still, as he rode away, he couldn't shake the feeling he was being watched.

CHAPTER 8

Found!

After dinner, the children were playing Go Fish when Grandma Belle's grandson called. "So sorry we missed your visit," he said, "but I took Grandma Belle to a doctor's appointment. Her hip is doing very well. She was feeling so much better that we decided to celebrate. We went to the Applewood Café for dinner."

Henry asked about the two-horned mask they found in the trash. "Don't know a thing about that, not a thing," said the grandson. "I never threw away anything like that. And no one else was home. Since we were going out, I gave Nurse Rumple the day off."

Henry thought about the red car he'd seen in the alley. He'd thought it was Nurse Rumple's, but he must have been wrong.

"Maybe," the grandson said, "a neighbor threw their trash in our can. That happens sometimes when people's cans get too full." He paused a moment. "We also have a small mystery. Our yard looks a bit different than when we left. Would you know anything about that?"

Henry, very proud of himself for helping Grandma Belle, explained that he'd cleared the weeds and trimmed the bushes. "Well, you might have checked with us first," said the grandson. He did not sound at all happy.

"D…don't you like it?" asked Henry.

"Yes, yes we do, very much so. It's just that Grandma Belle is still unhappy because Nurse Rumple has moved so many things from the house to the garage, and

Grandma Belle doesn't want anything else to change around here. It may seem odd to you, but Grandma likes her clutter. She finds it a comfort having her things around. Every time she asks, Nurse Rumple promises to bring everything back once Grandma Belle can get around the house a bit better. But Grandma is starting to get around just fine, and everything is still locked up in the garage." He sighed. "I'd move her things myself, but I have a bad back. The point is, people should ask before they do something for someone. Even when it's a nice thing. Don't you agree?"

Henry thought about Mrs. McGregor surprising them by cleaning the garage. She meant well, but she had cleaned away any clues the thief might have left. "Yes," he said, "I agree. And I promise to ask permission next time. Do you think I could talk to Grandma Belle?"

"I'm afraid I wore her out—she fell asleep the second we came home. But I know she'd love to have you visit tomorrow, perhaps late afternoon? The new nurse starts work then, and I'm sure Grandma would love her to meet all of you. I'll say goodbye to you now. I'm flying home tomorrow. I'm sad to leave Grandma, but my work is in California."

*****

Officer Morgan called early the next morning. "Could you do me a favor and bring that horned mask to Pleasant Valley Park around noon? I have some friends I'd like to show it to."

Henry promised he would, then went to tell the others. He found them in the yard, sitting around a table piled high with paints and colored paper and a basket of odds and ends Violet kept for art projects. "Come join us," she called, "we're making rainsticks."

Violet had one last *Prairie Girl* book, called *Thunderstick*, left on her bookshelf. "Each book teaches a craft you can do," she said. "Native Americans make rainsticks out of dead cactus plants. But since cactus doesn't grow here in Connecticut, we need to improvise."

"What's 'improvise'?" Benny asked.

"It means making do with what you have." Violet set out four paper towel tubes. "These will be our cacti." Then she put out a bag of dry beans and a bag of unpopped popcorn. Next she took a box of nails from Henry's tool box, and a roll of strong tape. She showed them how to tape one end of their tubes closed, then push two-inch nails into the tubes all around. "When you finish," said Violet, "the inside of your tube should look as if porcupines backed into it." They worked hard for a while, then looked into their tubes and saw a crisscross of nails.

"Now pour one cup of popcorn kernels or beans into your tubes and tape the tops closed." When they'd finished, Violet smiled and said, "Listen." Slowly, she turned her tube upside down. The hard popcorn kernels fell from the top of the tube to the bottom. *Plink, plink,* they sang as they hit the nails. *Plink, plink.*

"Rain!" cried Benny. "It sounds like rain!" They all practiced making rain sounds, then

finished their rainsticks by painting designs all around and gluing on decorations. Violet wrapped hers with strands of yarn. Benny glued blades of grass and weeping willow leaves on his. Henry dipped the Sunday comics in a mix of flour and water and wrapped the colorful pages around his tube. Jessie glued on beads from an old broken necklace. The children left the rainsticks out to dry and cleaned up their worktable. After lunch, they put the two-horned mask in Jessie's bike basket and rode toward town.

"Can we stop?" asked Benny as they passed an ice cream stand. "I brought my allowance." Of course, they all joined him, each child picking out something different. Henry always ate vanilla. Jessie tried a new flavor every time. Violet liked half chocolate and half strawberry. And Benny liked whatever had the most color. Today it was Bubblegum Burst. As they wandered down the sidewalk licking their cones, they passed Ye Olde Antique Shoppe. "This is the shop Nurse Rumple was coming out of the other day," said Jessie, "when she was yelling at the man in the orange truck."

Dozens of wonderful old things were crammed the display window.

"Look," said Benny, "that's just like my old yo-yo."

"And my comic books," said Henry.

"And my old figure skates," said Jessie

Violet gasped. "There's *Katrina and the Kachina Doll!*"

The children ran inside. The tiny shop was crammed full of books and dishes, toys and clothes—every shelf, table, countertop, and floor space covered. A woman glared at them from behind the counter. "No eating in the store," she said.

Violet took her book out of the window display, excitedly flipping through the pages. "Here," she said, pointing to a drawing of Prairie Girl Katrina holding a kachina doll.

"You mustn't touch the merchandise," the woman snapped.

"But you bought all of this from our yard sale," said Violet.

"Yes," said the woman, "and now it is mine. If you want it, you must buy it."

Violet stared at the price sticker on her book. "Fifteen dollars? But...I sold it to you for twenty-five cents!"

"That is why *I* am in business," the woman took the book, "and you are in school. These books are very old and—except for milk and tuna-salad sandwiches—the older something is, the more valuable it becomes. Now, outside, all of you."

The children walked out to finish their ice cream, watching as the woman dusted the items in the window display.

"Look," Benny pointed, "that's our can."

The Crispy Crackers can sat in the back of the display with old cans and tins and metal boxes. The children ran back inside. The woman glowered at them. "I thought I told you—"

"That can belongs to us," Jessie said.

"Which one?"

"That green one, way in back."

The woman folded her arms across her

chest. "That could be anyone's old can."

"No," said Jessie. "We can prove it's ours."

"It has black burn marks on the bottom," said Violet. "When we lived in the boxcar, we'd fill the can with water from the stream and set it on hot stones to heat water for washing and cooking."

"And," Henry said, "it's full of money."

"*What?*"

"Open it," said Jessie. "You'll see."

"It…it doesn't open." The woman's face turned bright red. "I tried. It's stuck shut."

"I can get it open," said Henry. And before she could stop him, he climbed into the display window and took out the can. Sure enough, the bottom of the can was burnt black. Using the heel of his shoe and a nail left over from his rain stick, Henry hammered off the lid. Dollar bills and coins spilled out. Benny quickly scurried around, picking them up.

"That can was just sitting out on a stump near that old boxcar," snapped the woman.

"Yes," said Jessie, her voice angry, "it was

sitting right next to the sign—the really BIG sign—that said 'Donations for the Homeless Shelter.'"

"There was no sign," she said, "just a dog and cat running around."

The children glanced at each other. They remembered Watch chasing the cat around the yard, knocking things over. "I guess Watch could have knocked the sign down," said Jessie. "Still, you shouldn't have taken the can without asking."

"Well, *you* told me that only items on the tables were for sale, and it didn't look like something that anyone would miss so I...I...I..." Tiny drops of sweat dotted the woman's upper lip. She patted her forehead with a handkerchief. "This was a terrible misunderstanding. I...I...I," she took a deep breath, "I apologize."

It seemed so hard for her to say that the children guessed she didn't apologize very often.

"Look!" cried Benny, pointing to an old wooden table piled high with dishes and silverware. He reached across the table and grabbed a silver candleholder from behind a stack of dishes. It was coated with orange and black wax. "That's Grandma Belle's candleholder! The one she used on Halloween."

Violet grabbed Henry's arm and pulled him to one side. "What if Grandma Belle's nurse didn't come here to buy something," she whispered. "What if she came here to sell?"

Henry thought this over. He took the candleholder from Benny and set it on the counter in front of the woman. "Where did you get this?" he asked.

The woman blinked, then blinked again. "Why, people bring things to sell all the time. I can hardly be expected to remember where all my treasures come from."

The children suspected she wasn't telling the truth. But she turned away and began dusting some shelves.

"What about my mask?" asked Benny. "Did you take it out of our garage?"

The woman whirled around. "I don't know anything about any mask," she said.

"And I want you children out of here, out of here *now*."

As the children walked out of the store with their green can, they had a feeling she knew exactly where Grandma Belle's candleholder had come from, and it was up to them to find out how it ended up in her store.

CHAPTER 9

Powwow

The children pedaled hard up the steep hill that overlooked Pleasant Valley Park. Suddenly, they came to a screeching halt. They barely recognized their favorite park in the large valley below. Gone were the baseball and soccer fields, the playgrounds and basketball courts. In their place, as far as the eye could see, was a city of white tepees. Excited, the children coasted down the hill to the park to join the fun. As they locked their bikes onto the bike stand, Benny carefully removed the mask from Jessie's bike basket.

It was hard to know where to look first. Children of all ages played a noisy game of tag, running in and out of tepees and all around the park. Long craft tables covered the toddler playground. At each one, people sewed moccasins or wove bright beads into bracelets and headbands. Small children glued feathers and beads onto leather strips that they tied around their arms and waists.

A group of people sat on the ground around a very old woman, watching as she carved beautiful designs into a black clay pot. And, oh, the delicious smells in the air! Even though their bellies were full of ice cream, the children knew they must sample some powwow foods before they left.

"This way," said Henry, walking along a row of open tents with banners reading: Food, Crafts, Storytelling.

A young woman at the information tent directed people this way and that. Violet studied the bead design on her dress so she could copy it. Sewing the beads would take many hours but, as Grandfather said, "A journey of a thousand miles begins with a single step." When it was their turn to speak to the woman, the children asked where they could find Officer Tom Morgan.

"Let's see," the woman checked a list of names. "Ah, yes, Tom's helping build the bonfire on the west end of the park." She pointed them toward an area set far away from the tents. The children headed over.

As they neared, they saw people piling logs, branches, and twigs in the shape of a square. The square was already as tall as Benny, and it looked as if it would be much taller before all the branches were used up.

They found Officer Morgan working with a group of teenagers. "Welcome," he said. "I'd like to show that mask of yours to one of the tribes here." He turned to the teenagers. "Keep building," he told them. "I'll be back to help in a little while."

He led the Aldens toward the largest tepee

in the park. "You are about to meet some very important tribe members," he said. "They have come from all over the United States for this powwow. I told them about the masks you found."

Inside the tent, a group of people sat in a circle. Some wore jeans and tee shirts, and others were dressed in clothing decorated with beads and feathers. Officer Morgan introduced the children. He turned to Benny. "Would you show them your mask?"

Benny took the mask out of its box and walked into the center of the circle. A man leaned forward as Benny lifted up the two-horned mask.

"Ahhhh," he said, taking it from him, passing it around the circle. Each held it and ran his hands along the old wood, admiring the talent of the artist who made it. When it had gone all the way around the circle, the last man spoke.

"This is a Hopi cow kachina mask. This spirit prays for rain and food for the Hopi people," he said. "The Hopi have not arrived

yet—if you will leave the mask, we will show it to them."

"No!" yelled Benny, grabbing the mask and clutching it to him. "I found it! It's mine!"

The man's voice was gentle. "That is true. You did find it. And you could take it home. But this mask is very old. It may have been stolen from the Hopi tribe." Benny clutched it tighter. The man looked at him with kind eyes. "It is a great honor—a great, great honor—to return a stolen thing to its true home."

Benny hugged his mask. He knew how sad he felt when the mask had been stolen from their garage. He also knew how happy he felt today when they found the missing Crispy Crackers can. He looked at the chiefs who sat quietly, watching him and waiting. No one yelled at him or grabbed the mask or told him what to do. They were waiting for him to decide. It made Benny feel very grown-up.

"All right," he said, handing the mask to

the man next to him.

"We would like to invite you to come back to the powwow on Saturday. By then we will know about the mask," the man said to the children.

On their way out of the park, the Aldens saw a group of people gathered around a table labeled "Fry bread."

"That's what Katrina ate in the *Prairie Girls* book," said Violet. "We should try it."

The children joined the line, watching a woman pull a small piece of dough off a big piece. She quickly rolled it into a ball, rolled it in flour, then patted it flat. Then she poked a hole in the middle. "The hole lets the oil get into the middle so the fry bread cooks evenly," explained Violet.

"Everyone stand back," said the woman. All the children took a giant step back as she dropped the dough into a large pan. Hot oil spattered like a Fourth-of-July sparkler. As the dough bubbled merrily in the hot oil, she added many more breads to the pan.

When they were done she scooped them

onto paper towels to drain. Some people ordered their fry bread plain, and some asked for regular sugar.

"I'm having powdered sugar," said Benny. When it was their turn, Henry, Jessie, and Violet all ordered the powdered sugar, too. The children sat under a large maple tree to enjoy their treats.

Officer Morgan found them there. "Thanks for leaving your mask, Benny," he said as he walked towards them.

"You're welcome," said Benny, who by now had a powdered-sugar moustache.

"We need to talk to Grandma Belle," Henry said. "If the people here think that this mask may belong to the Hopi tribe, then maybe there are other things that Grandma Belle has that need to be returned to these people."

"Do you think that Grandma Belle's father stole the masks from the Hopi tribe?" Benny asked.

"I don't know," said Henry. "But that's what we need to find out."

*****

As the children pedaled through town, they passed the drugstore. Down the block, Henry spotted the orange pickup truck they had seen in their alley parked in front of the diner.

"Something's wrong with that truck," said Henry.

"It's orange," said Violet, who much preferred softer colors.

Jessie wrinkled her nose. "It's all bumped and dented and has more rust than a sunken ship."

"No," said Henry, studying the truck. "I know what's wrong. Those are the same bikes and swing set in the back as before. Mr. Robbins would have sold them all by now, and collected all sorts of new things."

"You mean he's not a junker like Mr. Robbins?" asked Violet. "He's just pretending to be a junker?"

Henry nodded. "That way, people aren't suspicious when they see him driving up and down the alleys."

"Alleys like ours," said Benny, his face growing red with excitement. "He could have stolen my mask from our garage!"

"And maybe," said Jessie, "he stole things, like the candleholder, from Grandma Belle's garage. Maybe he's the one who took it to the antique store."

Henry jumped on his bike. "Quick! We have to get over to Grandma Belle's to let her know what's going on before anything else disappears."

CHAPTER 10

The Thief Unmasked!

The children pedaled so fast they were out of breath when they knocked on Grandma Belle's door. They waited, then knocked again. Nurse Rumple finally opened the door wearing rubber gloves and holding a giant bottle of cleaning spray. "Sssshh!" she said, smiling sweetly.

"We've come to see Grandma Belle," said Jessie.

"The dear lady is napping." The smell of

cleaning spray and fresh popcorn drifted out of the house. "She mustn't be disturbed. Please come back tomorrow." She shut the door.

"Did you smell the popcorn?" asked Jessie.

"If she's cleaning and Grandma Belle is napping, who is the popcorn for?" The children looked at each other.

Suddenly, Henry thought of something. "The popcorn isn't for eating, it's for packing! The nurse and the man in the truck are stealing from Grandma Belle!"

"I see," said Jessie. "The nurse packs up all of Grandma Belle's things and leaves them in the trash for the man in the orange truck to pick up."

"We did see them talking on the street," pointed out Violet.

"In front of the antique shop where we found Grandma Belle's candleholder," added Jessie.

"And we know the man in the truck isn't a real junker," said Benny.

Henry rang the bell again. It took Nurse

Rumple a long while to answer. "You again?" she asked, a little less sweetly than before.

"We need to see Grandma Belle," said Violet. "We have something very important we need to talk to her about."

"I told you she's napping." Nurse Rumple sprayed and wiped the brass mailbox next to the front door. "And I sent her grandson to pick up some medicine."

"We'll wait," said Jessie, trying to step inside. "We want to say goodbye to him."

Nurse Rumple blocked the doorway. "He won't have time. As soon as he drops off the medicine, he's catching a plane back to California." She sprayed cleaning spray on the doorknob and door and then briskly rubbed them with a rag. "The new nurse arrives in a few hours. It would be better if you came back then. Right now, I am the only one here." She held up the cleaning spray and sponge. "As you can see, I have work to do. I am very, *very* busy." She began closing the door.

Jessie stopped it with her hand. "We need

to borrow something," she said. "Grandma Belle's silver candleholder."

Nurse Rumple's face turned as white as her uniform. "I...I don't know what you're talking about."

"It's big," Jessie said, "and holds five candles."

"I've certainly never seen anything like that. It's probably out with all the other junk in the garage."

"Then will you let us into the garage," said Henry, "so we can look for it?"

"I...I don't have the key. Grandma Belle's grandson put it away someplace. Now, I have no time, no time at all. I insist you do not disturb us again." This time, when she shut the door, they heard the loud click of the lock.

The children walked down the front steps, but they didn't get on their bikes. "I don't trust Nurse Rumple alone with all of Grandma Belle's things," said Violet. "I don't want to leave here until her grandson comes back."

"Follow me," said Henry, walking quietly around the side of the house. "We need to take a look at that garage."

They peeked in the garage window. Every inch of space was crammed with old tables and chairs, dishes and silverware. White boxes were stacked near the door. A black clay pot rested inside a box on a bed of pop-corn. "That's like the pot the woman was making at the powwow today," said Violet.

Jessie burned with anger. "Nurse Rumple didn't move these from the house because they were too much clutter. She moved them so they'd be easier to steal!"

Suddenly, the back door to the house jerked open. "Quick!" Henry said, leading them across the alley where they hid behind a neighbor's garage. They peeked out as Nurse Rumple hurried to the garage carry-ing a green garbage bag. She unlocked the garage door and disappeared inside.

"She does have the garage key," said Benny. "She lied."

A few minutes later, Nurse Rumple carried

a white box out to a trash can and placed it gently inside. She went back into the garage and a minute later brought out two more white boxes to put in the trash. Pretty soon, the can was so full that the lid barely fit on the top of the can. Her cell phone rang.

"Yes?" she snapped. "What! He's done already? I thought I gave her grandson plenty of chores to keep him busy. All right, all right, get over here, now. Yes, right now! We have to get all of this stuff out of here before the new nurse comes. I'll keep him busy in the house until you pick up the goods." She hurried back up the walk to the house.

As soon as the back door closed, the children ran to the trash cans and peered inside. Every can was filled to the brim with white boxes. The trash cans smelled like fresh-popped corn.

"She's been stealing Grandma Belle's wonderful things," said Violet. "We have to stop her."

They ran around to the garage. In her hurry, Nurse Rumple had left the door unlocked. The children quickly ducked inside. They heard a truck rumble down the alley and stop outside the garage. Henry peered out the small window. "It's the orange truck," he whispered. "He and Nurse Rumple *are* working together."

Jessie jumped up. "I'm going to call Officer Morgan."

Henry grabbed her arm. "Tell him to get here right away."

"Please hurry!" said Violet.

Jessie took off, running at top speed through the yard, cutting across to where they'd seen the mother and toddler out in front. The others watched, not daring to breathe until she was safely out of sight.

Benny climbed up on an old box, trying to see out the window. He watched the man with the beard climb out of the truck and walk to the trash cans. Suddenly, the box crumpled under him and Benny fell with a loud thud. The driver stopped, tilting his head, listening. The children ducked down, freezing like statues under the window.

What if the man came into the garage? What if he found them? Henry crawled to the door. He quietly pushed it closed, turning the lock good and tight. He crawled back under the window, and pressed his back against the wall to huddle down with the others.

Heavy footsteps. Someone brushed against the window! The children felt sure he could hear their hearts beating. Sunshine behind the man cast his shadow as he peered in. The shadow looked left, then right. After a few moments, it disappeared. The children stared at the doorknob. It jerked left and right, left and right. For a moment everything went still, then footsteps tramped back around the garage and out to the alley.

They listened to the clatter of trash can lids, the opening and closing of the pickup truck doors. "Do you think Jessie reached Officer Morgan?" whispered Violet. The truck engine roared, and the pickup drove off.

"Oh, no," said Benny. "He's getting away!"

In a flash, Henry unlocked the door and yanked it open, just as Nurse Rumple banged a suitcase down the back stairs.

"What!" She gasped, staring at Henry. "What are you doing here?"

"Hide," Henry whispered to the others. Violet and Benny ducked behind an old chair. Henry stood guarding the doorway.

"Get out!" yelled Nurse Rumple, hurrying toward the garage, clacking the suitcase behind her. "Get out of my garage!"

"This is not your garage," Henry said.

"Don't you talk back to me, young man," she said, wagging a finger in his face. "Don't you—"

"Go!" shouted Henry. Violet and Benny jumped from behind the chair and dashed past Nurse Rumple, not stopping until they were inside Grandma Belle's house. They quickly locked the door.

Nurse Rumple spun around, not sure where to turn first. "You…you little thieves. I'll call the police. I'll—"

"Yes," said Henry. "Call the police. In fact,

you don't have to. My sister has already taken care of that."

With that news, Nurse Rumple turned and ran across the backyard. In seconds, four Greenfield police cars—their sirens blaring—squealed up to the house with Officer Morgan's car close behind. Henry dashed to the front. "She went that way!" he yelled as he directed the police through the backyard.

Benny ran to Officer Morgan. "You have to hurry," he said. "The man in the orange truck is getting away."

"An orange truck should be easy enough to find." Officer Morgan phoned in an alert.

Grandma Belle's grandson pulled into the driveway. He looked very frightened.

"What's wrong? Why are the police here? Has something happened to Grandma?"

"I'm fine, dear, I'm fine." Grandma Belle smiled, waving as Violet pushed her wheelchair onto the porch. "I napped right through all the excitement. Thank goodness these wonderful children were here."

The police returned with the nurse in

handcuffs. "Found her trying to escape down the alley on the next block," one of them said, leading her away.

"Where are they taking Nurse Rumple?" asked the grandson.

"She's no nurse," said Benny. "She's a thief!"

"That she is," said Officer Morgan. "My friend has been on her trail all week."

Violet stared at the man climbing out of Officer Morgan's car, the man with the braid down his back and the silver bracelet. "Children," said Officer Morgan. "I'd like you to meet Ahote, chief detective of the Hopi tribal police."

*****

It was Benny's idea to serve Nurse Rumple's big bag of popcorn. "I know I can't eat packing corn because it's stale," he said, "but this was just popped." The children quickly arranged a picnic on Grandma Belle's front porch. Violet poured everyone an ice-cold glass of water just as Grandma Belle's grandson came out of the house.

"I'm staying for a few days," he said, "just to be sure you're all right."

Ahote came around from the garage, pulling a wagon filled with Hopi treasures. He sat on the steps next to the children.

"You have done something very important, today," he told them. "Rumple and her brother, the man in the orange truck, are wanted by police in eight states. She pretends to be a nurse and finds jobs taking care of people like Grandma Belle. Then she and her brother steal everything they can, and move on. She never left fingerprints, so the police didn't know who she was."

"That's why she was scrubbing everything," said Jessie, "to erase her fingerprints."

Ahote nodded. "I came to Greenfield for the powwow and saw one of our sacred masks in an antique shop window. The owner wouldn't tell me where she got it until I showed her my police badge. She found the receipt but it had no name or address, just 'Locust Street.' The shop owner gave me the mask in a white box. I decided to drive along Locust, and I saw you pulling a white box in your wagon. I followed you."

"You came to our yard sale looking for more masks," said Benny.

"Yes. Your sister said you'd had a mask for sale but by the time I came it was gone. I thought you'd sold it."

"No. I wanted to keep it," said Benny. "I put it in the garage. But then it was stolen."

"By the man in the orange truck," Henry decided. "Watch, our dog, must have tried to stop him. He chased the thief around the garage, then into the alley. I think the thief threw the box with the popcorn at Watch to keep him busy long enough for him to escape."

"Did you really think we were selling stolen kachinas?" asked Violet.

Ahote's cheeks reddened. "The evidence did point that way. Luckily, you caught the real thief."

"I feel so silly," said Grandma Belle. She looked lovingly at the beautiful items in the wagon. "I never even suspected what was going on."

"Rumple was very good at what she did," said Officer Morgan. "She's fooled many people over many years."

Gently, Ahote took Grandma Belle's hand. "Your father's collection—the kachina masks and clay pots—did not belong to him. They belonged—they still belong—to the Hopi people."

The old woman's eyes grew wet with tears. "He didn't know. He was just a young boy, playing in the land near his home. He found things the way any child might. My father was a good and honest man. He would never keep something that belonged to someone else. Nor would he want me to. She patted Ahote's hand. "Please take back everything that is yours. And, tell the people from your tribe that we meant no harm."

*****

The powwow was one of the greatest days ever! Grandfather came, and Grandma Belle and her grandson. The children walked along with Officer Morgan, taking a taste of every food Benny brought them. Violet spent the afternoon making a beaded necklace, and Jessie learned to shoot a bow and arrow. Henry entered a footrace that went all around the park three times. He came in tenth place, which was very good for a boy of fourteen.

Finally, it grew dark. "I must go," said Grandma Belle. "I've decided to live with my grandson in California." She smiled at Henry. "When I saw how beautiful you made my garden, I realized my house needs young people to care for it. You are all invited to come for a visit as soon as you can."

They promised they would, then went to meet Ahote and the Hopi elders around the great bonfire. "I'll be right there," said Henry, running to Grandfather's car and returning with a large bag.

"Thank you for returning our treasures to us," said Ahote. "The elders asked me to invite you to sit next to us."

As the bonfire sparks flew up into the

night sky, the children watched many dances and listened to beautiful songs. It was late when Grandfather said it was time to go.

"Just one minute," said Violet. Although she was usually shy in crowds, she took the bag from Henry and stood in front of Ahote and the Hopi tribe. "We would like to give these gifts to you," she said. And, with that, she opened the bag and took out the rainsticks the children had made.

"These are wonderful gifts," said Ahote. "We promise to use them. Back home in Arizona it has been a very dry season, even for the desert. We need rain."

Benny jumped up. "Let me show you how they work," he said, turning his rainstick slowly until the popcorn kernels fell down against the nails. "See, it sounds like rain."

Suddenly, they heard the long low rumble of distant thunder.

"Oh," said Benny. The others tried not to laugh as he quickly put down the rainstick. "M...m...maybe," he said softly, "you should put these away until you get back home."

GERTRUDE CHANDLER WARNER discovered when she was teaching that many readers who like an exciting story could find no books that were both easy and fun to read. She decided to try to meet this need, and her first book, *The Boxcar Children*, quickly proved she had succeeded.

Miss Warner drew on her own experiences to write the mystery. As a child she spent hours watching trains go by on the tracks opposite her family home. She often dreamed about what it would be like to set up housekeeping in a caboose or freight car—the situation the Alden children find themselves in.

While the mystery element is central to each of Miss Warner's books, she never thought of them as strictly juvenile mysteries. She liked to stress the Aldens' independence and resourcefulness and their solid New England devotion to using up and making do. The Aldens go about most of their adventures with as little adult supervision as possible—something else that delights young readers.

Miss Warner lived in Putnam, Connecticut, until her death in 1979. During her lifetime, she received hundreds of letters from girls and boys telling her how much they liked her books.